People Around Town
MEET THE CONSTRUCTION WORKER

By Joyce Jeffries

Gareth Stevens
Publishing

Please visit our website, www.garethstevens.com. For a free color catalog of all our high-quality books, call toll free 1-800-542-2595 or fax 1-877-542-2596.

Library of Congress Cataloging-in-Publication Data

Jeffries, Joyce.
Meet the construction worker / by Joyce Jeffries.
   p. cm. – (People around town)
Includes index.
ISBN 978-1-4339-9362-6 (pbk.)
ISBN 978-1-4339-9363-3 (6-pack)
ISBN 978-1-4339-9364-0 (library binding)
1. Construction workers—Juvenile literature. 2. Occupations—Juvenile literature. I. Jeffries, Joyce. II. Title.
TH149.J44 2013
624—dc23

First Edition

Published in 2014 by
Gareth Stevens Publishing
111 East 14th Street, Suite 349
New York, NY 10003

Copyright © 2014 Gareth Stevens Publishing

Editor: Ryan Nagelhout
Designer: Nicholas Domiano

Photo credits: Cover, p. 1 Diego Cervo/Shutterstock.com; p. 5 Iakov Filimonov/Shutterstock.com; p. 7 Anton Gvozdikov/Shutterstock.com; pp. 9, 15, 17 iStockphoto/Thinkstock.com; p. 11 ivvvv1975/Shutterstock.com; pp. 13, 21 Brand X Pictures/Thinkstock.com; p. 24 Africa Studio/Shutterstock.com; p. 19 Huntstock/Thinkstock.com; p. 23 pryzmat/Shutterstock.com; p. 24 (hammer) ILYA AKINSHIN/Shutterstock.com, (nails) Africa Studio/Shutterstock.com, (saw) Andrey Eremin/Shutterstock.com.

Printed in the United States of America

CPSIA compliance information: Batch #CS13GS: For further information contact Gareth Stevens, New York, New York at 1-800-542-2595.

Contents

Construction workers build your town!

They make
big buildings.

Many drive big trucks.

They use a crane
to lift heavy things.

They cut wood
with a saw.

13

They hit things
with a hammer.
These are nails.

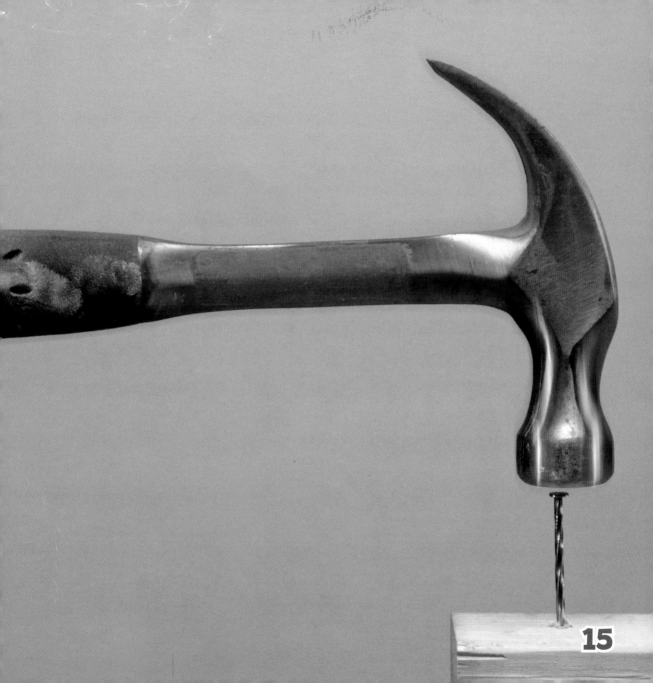

15

They wear yellow hats.
These keep them safe!

Some work with wood.
These are called
carpenters.

Some put on the top
of your home.
These are roofers.

Others bring your house water.
These are pipe fitters.

23

Words to Know

hammer

nails

saw

Index